This World is Beautiful

Rabindranath Tagore
A Collection for Young People

Rabindranath Tagore (1861-1941) is known mainly in the West for translations of his verse and as a painter who exhibited in Europe and America, although in his native Bengal he is famous as the composer of more than two thousand songs, as a novelist, playwright and short story writer, and as an educator who was both original and far-seeing.

It has been a difficult task to choose excerpts from his work to convey to new readers the scope of his writing. We hope that this unusual and varied collection will go a long way towards meeting the demands of any young person who would like to make contact with such an imaginative and enlightened man.

The TAGORE CENTRE (U.K.) is making available to English speaking readers some of the best creative works of another country and in so doing builds a cultural bridge between the West and India.

THIS WORLD
IS
BEAUTIFUL

This World is Beautiful

RABINDRANATH TAGORE

A COLLECTION
FOR YOUNG PEOPLE

The Tagore Centre U.K.
Alexandra Park Library
Alexandra Park Road
London N22 4UJ

1988

First published: 1988
Reprinted: 1993

This World is Beautiful was prepared for publication by Sakti Bhattacharya, Kalyan Kundu, Jill Parvin and Kalyan Sircar, who worked together as a team participating equally in its production.

Acknowledgement

We are grateful to Setareh Campbell who designed the cover and advised on presentations; to photographers, Sunil Janah (Bengal landscape) and Hannah Lee (Tagore workshop); to William Radice for his advice and encouragement; to Lionel Jones and Camelot Press for their active support throughout the project, and GLA for making the whole thing possible.

ISBN Number 0951336800

This project is funded by Greater London Arts

Printed and Bound in Britain by Redwood Books,
Trowbridge Wilts

CONTENTS

ILLUSTRATIONS

Introduction

To ask questions about Rabindranath Tagore is to invite more questions and still more. The list of his accomplishments, achievements, endeavours, is endless; there is scarcely an area in which he did not excel. At first sight this may be utterly daunting as we cannot help feeling amazed at his continued energy and enthusiasms. Yet maybe this is the very reason why we should in 1988 suggest to young people who read English that it would be a good idea to become interested in a man who lived in Bengal between 1861 and 1941. Rabindranath Tagore interested himself in people everywhere even at a time when nationalism was the predominant force in the world so maybe we should return the compliment. Late in the twentieth century we can learn from him, as well as enjoy the varied works of such a gifted man.

Rabindranath was born into a large and very talented family. Music, dance, drama, literature and painting were present everywhere and the boy flourished in this atmosphere, enjoying endless hours composing and writing. Friends of the family, together with his brothers and sisters, encouraged him generously and in his early years he wrote many songs which later became famous throughout Bengal. His trips to England, as a young man, were a source of great enjoyment and he observed with humour and interest the differences between India and this country noting with pleasure and hardly any annoyance, that people expressed more surprise at his customs than he would have dreamed of expressing at theirs!

Relieved when he came home to learn that there would be no pressure to become a lawyer, Tagore entered with enthusiasm into a life in which he managed the family estates and more importantly became an established poet and story-teller. His observation of the rural life around him was poured into his writing, and all his songs, stories and poems reflect a sense of urgency to be at one with his own people and, later, with the people of the world. This humanity, together with his innovatory strength in the arts, placed him at the centre of the cultural renaissance in the India of that time.

His creative energy was further poured into the making of a school, Santiniketan—Abode of Peace—which became the model for Dartington Hall (Totnes, Devon) run by his friend and associate Leonard Elmhirst. His school grew in size and reputation and Visva-Bharati—the University of the World—was established to extend his influence still further by encouraging the learning of both Arts and Sciences in an atmosphere of peace, yet awareness of the problems of the world.

In the early years of this century he actively supported the popular movement against the partition of Bengal, proposed by the British. He later made clear his objections to violence and condemned terrorism as a means to win India's freedom. In his contribution to the Nationalist struggle he always emphasized the need for reform and regeneration in Indian society.

At about this time he began translating his works into English and, following a visit to England where he met William Rothenstein, who like Elmhirst became a great friend, some of his poems were published as *Gitanjali—Song Offerings* (1912). The immediate acclaim of this volume led to his receiving the Nobel Prize for literature.

In 1915 he was Knighted, only to renounce that title four years later when he protested fiercely at the massacre, by British troops at Amritsar, of unarmed civilians.

More than ever stirred by his desire for international peace, he travelled the world in the 1920s and '30s seeking the essential key to unity and freedom.

In 1924 he turned to painting. The rhythm and form essential to his writing found expression in his painting. Strange landscapes, bizarre creatures, faces which tell tales wild and still, of both anguish and resignation, all reveal through visual image the turbulent world of his imagination and his never-ending search for harmony. "The world of form, it strikes me, must be a dream world conjured up by our Creator, manifold in its lives and colours," Tagore wrote.

He received a Doctorate from the University of Oxford in August 1940. A year later, while still involved actively both in writing and in plans for his own University, he died in Calcutta, on 7th August, 1941, to be remembered with enormous affection and respect by his fellow Indians and by those other nations fortunate enough to know his works.

In both its title and content this volume reflects Rabindranath's own thoughts and beliefs; his work proclaims 'This World is Beautiful'.

Dates

1861 Rabindranath born in Calcutta on 7th May.

1869 He begins to write poetry.

1874 Translations of Macbeth into Bengali; first publication of a poem in a popular journal in Calcutta.

1875 Death of his mother.

1878 First visit to England.

1879 Admitted to London University.

1880 Returns to India before completing his studies.

1881 First public address – 'Music and Moods'. Second visit to England.

1883 Marries Mrinalini Devi.

1888 First translation of one of his poems in English is published.

1889 Starts to look after his estates at Selaidah.

1890 Comes to England, returns via Paris.

1891 Travels throughout India.

1898 Prayer hall at Santiniketan opened. Appointed as editor of 'Bharati' a literary journal published in Calcutta.

1901 Starts his own school at Santiniketan with only five students.

1902 Death of his wife.

1905 Death of his father. He protests openly against the Bill of Partition of Bengal, proposed by Lord Curzon.

1907 His younger son, Samindra dies.

1910 Publishes 'Gitanjali' in Bengali. House built for Santiniketan School – Abode of Peace.

1912 Comes to England with his translation of 'Gitanjali', which is published by India Society, London. Visit to U.S.A.

1913 Lecture at Chicago University and Harvard University. Awarded Nobel Prize for Literature.

1915 Spends time at Selaidah. Receives Gandhi and his wife at Santiniketan. Knighted by George V.

1916 Visits Japan for the first time. Lectures on 'Nationalism and the Personality' in America.

1918 His eldest daughter Bela dies.

1919 Renunciation of his knighthood in protest at Amritsar massacre.

1921 Travels in America, England, France, Holland and Belgium. Lectures at Harvard. Inauguration of Visva-Bharati, the University at Santiniketan.

1924 Visits China and Japan. First visit to Latin America where he begins to paint. Meets Victoria O'Campo in Buenos Aires.

1926 World tour.

1929 Visit to Canada and Japan.

1930 Visit to England. Delivers Hibbert lectures at Oxford. First exhibition of his paintings in Paris, London, Birmingham and other European cities.

1940 Oxford University confers Doctorate on Tagore.

1941 Rabindranath Tagore dies in Calcutta on 7th August at the age of eighty.

LETTERS

LETTERS FROM EUROPE

The First encounter 1878

Before I came to England, I supposed that it was such a small island and its inhabitants were so devoted to higher culture that from one end to the other it would resound with the strains of Tennyson's lyre. I imagined that wherever I stayed on that tiny handful of land I would hear Gladstone's oratory, Max Muller's exegesis, Carlyle's deep reflections; . . . that wherever I went, one and all would be enthusiasts for intellectual pleasure. But I was very disappointed. Women attend to their appearance; men do their work; life goes on much as it does everywhere else—only in the political sphere is there a little more excitement . . .

. . . Gradually I am getting to know a few people here. One curious thing that I've noticed: people seem to think I am a complete ignoramous. They think that I have just come from India, that I don't know anything, that things therefore need to be shown and explained to me. One day I went out for a walk along the streets with Dr. M—'s brother, and was quite infuriated by him. There were some photographs in a shop window: he supposed that I would be absolutely amazed at the sight of the photographs—that my eyes would pop out of my head: he took me over to them and started to explain them to me laboriously. He told me that they were made by a machine, not drawn by a human hand. Quite a crowd gathered around us, and I was very embarrassed. I told him clearly that I was not unaware of what he was telling me. But did he believe me? Taking me on to a watch-shop, he tried to tell me what wonderful inventions watches are. He thought he was doing me a favour, but I was fuming! At an evening party, a young lady asked me if I had ever heard the sound of a piano . . .

At a Fancy Dress Ball

. . . I dressed up as a Bengali *zamindar*, clothes and *pugree* made of velvet stitched with gold thread—the lot! Some friends had got together and persuaded me to put on a false beard and moustache. But there is a god who punishes us for vanity, and the humiliation I suffered can barely be spoken or heard. None of the lovely lady-friends to whom I had been introduced before were willing to acknowledge me in my beard and moustache. They shook hands with everyone—shook hands with every other gentleman—but they paid no attention to poor me. Any that I approached shied away. I was so enraged and grieved and mortified and generally disgusted with myself, that there and then I pulled off the beard and moustache and stuffed them into my pocket. Things went better after that . . .

. . . Twirling round and round like a madman with an unknown girl is not my favourite way of being polite. It's not too bad dancing with those that I know well. There was one girl I knew, nice to look at, and I danced the Gallop with her without making too many mistakes. But the girl I danced the Lancers with I had never met before, and she was awful to look at: her eyes were bulbous, her cheeks were fat, her chin almost non-existent, and on top of all that she had a petulant disposition—when I danced with her everything possible went wrong . . . This girl probably wished me dead as she danced with me. When the dance ended I drew breath thankfully, and she must have been as glad to be released. Once I had to dance with a really beautiful partner: I did my best to avoid dancing with her, but the hostess especially asked me to dance, and in the end I was forced to take the floor. God knows how I managed!

At a Social Gathering

. . . As soon as one lady had finished her playing, the hostess began to press me to sing a song. This put me in a terrible jam. I knew that the people there did not have any great love for the songs of my country. The host and hostess had both heard me sing before, and had found my singing highly comical. They found it so amusing, that they went home and made up their minds that at the coming party this black-skinned Indian would have to caterwaul—thereby giving the assembled company a special "treat". I knew all this in my mind, but how can one dishonour the rules of

politeness? I might have indeed done so, had not Miss H— said in her sweet seductive voice, "Yes, do give us a song Mr. T.!" Mr. T. then without wasting any words gave a couple of coughs by way of introducing his song. The whole company fell silent. I began to wonder which song to sing. How could I sing the songs I truly love? I couldn't bear to think of everyone laughing at those songs. I began to sing a song. I have never been in such a frightful situation in all my life: somehow or other I managed to drag a few notes and a string of words out of my throat. The assembled ladies, whether Miss or Mrs, found this so funny that the stream of their amusement began to overwhelm the bounds of courtesy: they could not disguise their laughter—some of them turned their laughter into coughs, some of them tried to hide it by bending down, pretending that they had dropped something, one of them resorted to burying her face in her neighbour's back; even those who managed to retain their composure sent telegraph signals to each other with their eyes. The elderly lady who had previously shown off her musical talent displayed such sweet contempt and condescension in her smile that my blood froze when I saw her. You can well imagine what agony this was for a well-meaning fellow such as myself. By the time I got to the end of the song my face and ears had turned red, but because of my dark skin no one could see this. There was tumultuous applause all round, but after so much laughter I couldn't give much credence to it. The younger Miss H—asked me for an English translation of the song—the song was "*premer kathā ār bolo nā*"—"Do not speak any more of love". When she had heard it she asked me so that everyone could hear: "Is there free love in your country?" How on earth could such an idea have reached someone who did not know whether the people of India wore hats and coats or not, whether they spoke English from birth or not, or whether they went skating on the ice in winter or not! I was in such a state of mortification that I could only mumble incoherently. What is more, that evening I had to sing *twice*.

GLIMPSES OF BENGAL

12th December, 1895.

The other evening I was reading an English book of criticisms, full of all manner of disputations about Poetry, Art, Beauty, and so forth and so on. As I plodded through these artificial discussions, my tired faculties seemed to have wandered into a region of empty mirage, filled with the presence of a mocking demon.

The night was far advanced. I closed the book with a bang and flung it on the table. Then I blew out the lamp with the idea of turning into bed. No sooner had I done so than, through the open windows, the moonlight burst into the room, with a shock of surprise.

That little bit of a lamp had been sneering drily at me, like some Mephistopheles: and that tiniest sneer had screened off this infinite light of joy issuing forth from the deep love which is in all the world. What, forsooth, had I been looking for in the empty wordiness of the book? There was the very thing itself, filling the skies, silently waiting for me outside, all these hours!

If I had gone off to bed leaving the shutters closed, and thus missed this vision, it would have stayed there all the same without any protest against the mocking lamp inside. Even if I had remained blind to it all my life—letting the lamp triumph to the end—till for the last time I went darkling to bed—even then the moon would have still been there, sweetly smiling, unperturbed and unobtrusive, waiting for me as she has throughout the ages.

LETTER TO THE VICEROY

29th May, 1919.

The enormity of the measures taken by the Government in the Punjab for quelling some local disturbances has , with a rude shock, revealed to our minds the helplessness of our position as British subjects in India. The disproportionate severity of the punishments inflicted upon the unfortunate people and the methods of carrying them out, we are convinced, are without parallel in the history of civilized governments, barring some conspicuous exceptions, recent and remote. Considering that such treatment has been meted out to a population, disarmed and resourceless, by a power which has the most terribly efficient organization for destruction of human lives, we must strongly assert that it can claim no political expediency, far less moral justification. The accounts of the insults and sufferings undergone by our brothers in the Punjab have trickled through the gagged silence, reaching every corner of India, and the universal agony of indignation roused in the hearts of our people has been ignored by our rulers—possibly congratulating themselves for imparting what they imagine as salutary lessons . . . The very least I can do for my country is to take all consequences upon myself in giving voice to the protest of the millions of my countrymen, surprised into a dumb anguish of terror. The time has come when badges of honour make our shame glaring in the incongruous context of humiliation, and I for my part wish to stand, shorn of all special distinctions, by the side of those of my countrymen who for their so-called insignificance are liable to suffer degradation not fit for human beings.

LETTER TO A FRIEND

ANTWERP,
October 3rd, 1920.

I have spent about a fortnight in Holland. This fortnight has been most generous in its gifts to me. Of one thing you may be sure, that a communication of heart has been opened up between this little country and Santiniketan; and it remains with us to widen it and make use of it for the interchange of spiritual wealth. Altogether, Europe has come closer to us by this visit of ours. I only wish that all my friends in Santiniketan could realize how true this is and what a wealth it represents. Now I know more clearly than ever before that Santiniketan belongs to the world and we have to be worthy of this great fact. It is extremely difficult for us Indians to forget all the irritations that ever keep our consciousness concentrated on our own daily annoyances. But emancipation of consciousness is both the means and end of spiritual life. Therefore Santiniketan must be saved from the whirlwind of our dusty politics.

I am writing this letter from Antwerp, where I came yesterday morning; and I am getting ready to go to Brussels, where I have an invitation. And then I go to Paris.

LETTERS FROM RUSSIA

. . . 1930.

. . . What I see at present strikes me with wonder. Education is the biggest of all problems. So long the majority of the people had been denied full facilities for education, which in India is almost wholly denied; one cannot help feeling surprised to see how education here is being spread at all levels of the society with surprising enthusiasm. What impresses me is not only the number covered by education but its comprehensive character and the speed with which this is taking place . . .

. . . What I liked most here is the complete disappearance of the coarse pride in wealth. For this single reason the sense of self-respect of the common man has developed without impediment. All under-privileged groups like the farmer and labourer have been able to stand up with an erect head after shaking off the crushing weight of the pride of the privileged. I have been as much surprised as pleased to notice this.

REMINISCENCES

MY BOYHOOD DAYS

The Calcutta where I was born was an altogether old-world place. Hackney carriages lumbered about the city raising clouds of dust and the whips fell on the backs of skinny horses where bones showed plainly below their hide. There were no trams then, no buses, no motors. Business was not the breathless rush that it is now, and the days went by in leisurely fashion. Clerks would take a good pull at the *hookāh* before starting for office, and chew their betel as they went along. Some rode in palanquins, others joined in groups of four or five to hire a carriage in common, which was known as a "share-carriage". Wealthy men had monograms painted on their carriages, and a leather hood over the rear portion, like a half-drawn veil. The coachman sat on the box with his turban stylishly tilted to one side, and two grooms rode behind, girdles of yaks' tails round their waists, startling the pedestrians from their paths with their shouts of "Hey-yo!"

Women used to go about in the stifling darkness of closed palanquins; they shrank from the idea of riding in carriages, and even to use an umbrella in sun or rain was considered unwomanly. Any woman who was so bold as to wear the new-fangled bodice, or shoes on her feet, was scornfully nicknamed "mem-sahib", that is to say, one who had cast off all sense of propriety or shame. If any woman unexpectedly encountered a strange man, one outside her family circle, her veil would promptly descend to the very tip of her nose, and she would at once turn her back on him. The palanquins in which women went out were shut as closely as their apartments in the house.

An additional covering, a kind of thick tilt, completely enveloped the palanquin of a rich man's daughters and daughters-in-law, so that it looked like a moving tomb. By its side went the *durwan* carrying his brass-bound stick. His work was to sit in the entrance and watch the house, to tend his beard, safely to conduct the money to the bank and the women to their relatives' houses, and on festival days to dip the lady of the house into the Ganges, closed palanquin and all. Hawkers who came to the door with their array of wares would grease Shivnandan's palm to gain admission, and the drivers of hired carriages were also a source of profit to him. Sometimes a man who was unwilling to fall in with the idea of tipping the *durwan* would create a great scene in front of the porch.

Our *jamādār* Sobharam, who was a wrestler, used to spend a good deal of time in practising his preparatory feints and approaches, and in brandishing his heavy clubs. Sometimes he would sit and grind hemp for drink, and sometimes he would be quietly eating his raw radishes, tender leaves and all, when we boys would creep upon him and yell "Radha-Krishna!" in his ear. The more he waved his arms and protested the more we delighted in teasing him. And perhaps—who knows?—his protests were merely a cunning device for hearing repeated the name of his favourite god.

There was no gas then in the city, and no electric light. When the kerosene lamp was introduced, its brilliance amazed us. In the evening the house-servants lit castor-oil lamps in every room. The one in our study-room had two wicks in a glass bowl. . . .

The palanquin belonged to the days of my grand-mother. It was of ample proportions and lordly appearance. It was big enough to have needed eight bearers for each pole. But when the former wealth and glory of the family had faded like the glowing clouds of sunset, the palanquin-bearers, with their gold bracelets, their thick ear-rings, and their sleeveless red tunics, had disappeared along with it. The body of the palanquin had been decorated with coloured line drawings some of which were now defaced. Its surface was stained and discoloured, and the coir stuffing was coming out of the upholstery. It lay in a corner of the counting-house verandah as though it were a piece of commonplace lumber. I was seven or eight years old at that time.

I was not yet, therefore, of an age to put my hand to any serious work in the world, and the old palanquin on its part had been dismissed from all useful service. Perhaps it was this fellow-feeling that so much attracted me towards it. It was to me an island in the midst of the ocean, and on my holidays I became Robinson Crusoe. There I sat within its closed doors, completely lost to view, delightfully safe from prying eyes.

Outside my retreat, our house was full of people, innumerable relatives and other folk. From all parts of the house I could hear the shouts of the various servants at their work. Pyari the maid is returning from the bazaar through the front courtyard with her vegetables in a basket on her hip. Dukhon the bearer is carrying in Ganges water in a yoke across his shoulder. The weaver woman has gone into the inner apartments to trade the newest style of *sāris*. Dinu the goldsmith, who receives a monthly wage, usually sits in the room next to the lane, blowing his bellows and carrying out the orders of the family; now he is coming to the counting-house to present his bill to Kailas Mukherji, who has a quill pen stuck over his ear. The carder sits in the courtyard clearing the cotton mattress stuffing on his twanging bow. Mukundalal the durwan is rolling on the ground outside with the one-eyed wrestler, trying out a new wrestling fall. He slaps his thighs loudly, and repeats his physical jerks twenty or thirty times, dropping on all fours. There is a crowd of beggars sitting, waiting for their regular dole.

The day wears on, the heat grows intense, the clock in the gate-house strikes the hour. But inside the palanquin the day does not acknowledge the authority of clocks. Our midday is that of former days, when the drum at the gate door of the king's palace would be beaten for the breaking-up of the court, and the king would go to bathe in sandal-scented water. At midday on holidays those in charge of me have their meal and go to sleep. I sit on alone. My palanquin, outwardly at rest, travels on its imaginary journeys. My bearers, sprung from airy nothing at my bidding, eating the salt of my imagination, carry me wherever my fancy leads. We pass through far, strange lands, and I give each country a name from the books I have read. My imagination has cut a road through a deep forest. Tiger's eyes blaze from the thickets, my flesh creeps and tingles. With me is Visvanath the hunter; his gun cracks: boom!—and there, all is still. Sometimes my palanquin becomes a peacock-boat, floating far out on the ocean till the shore is out of sight. The oars fall into the water with a gentle splash, the waves swing and swell around us. The sailors cry to us to beware, a storm is coming. By the tiller stands Abdul the sailor, with his pointed beard, shaven moustache and close-cropped head. I know him, he brings hilsa fish and turtle eggs from the Padma for my elder brother.

Abdul has a story for me. One day at the end of *Chaitra* he had gone out in a dinghy to catch fish when there arose a great *Vaiśākh* gale. It was a tremendous typhoon and the boat sank lower and lower. Abdul seized the tow-rope in his teeth and jumping into the water swam to the shore, where he pulled his dinghy up after him by the rope. But the story comes to an end far too quickly for my taste, and besides, the boat is not lost, everything is saved—that isn't what I call a story! Again and again I demand, "What next?" "Well", says Abdul at last, "after that there were great doings. What should I see next but a panther with enormous whiskers. During the storm he had climbed up a *pākud* tree on the village *ghāt* on the other side of the river. In the violent wind the tree broke and fell into the Padma. Brother Panther came floating down on the current, rolled over and over in the water and reached and climbed the bank on my side. As soon as I saw him I made a noose of my tow-rope. The wild beast drew near, his big eyes glaring. He had grown very hungry with swimming, and when he saw me saliva dribbled from his red, lolling tongue. But, though he had known many other men inside and out, he did not know Abdul. I shouted to him, 'Come on, old boy', and as soon as he raised his fore-feet for the attack I dropped the noose around his neck. The more he struggled to get free the tighter grew the noose, until his tongue began to loll out. . . ." I am tremendously excited. "He didn't die, did he, Abdul?" I ask.

"Die?" says Abdul, "he couldn't die for the life of him. Well, the river was in spate, and I had to get back to Bahadurganj. I yoked my young panther to the dinghy and made him tow me fully forty miles. Oh, he might roar and snarl, but I goaded him on with my oar, and he carried me a ten or fifteen hours' journey in an hour and a half! Now, my little fellow, don't ask me what happened next, for you won't get an answer."

"All right," say I, "so much for the panther; now for the crocodile?" Says Abdul, "I have often seen the tip of his nose above the water. And how wickedly he smiles as he lies basking in the sun, stretched at full length on the shelving sandbanks of the river. If I'd had a gun I should have made his acquaintance. But my license has expired. . . .

Still, I can tell you one good yarn. One day Kanchi the gypsy woman was sitting on the bank of the river trimming bamboo with a bill-hook, with her young goat tethered nearby. All at once the crocodile appeared on the surface, seized the billy-goat by the leg and dragged it into the water. With one jump the gypsy woman landed astride on its back, and began sawing with her sickle at the throat of 'demon lizard', over and over again. The beast let off the goat and plunged into the water. . . ."

"And then? And then?" comes my excited question. "Why," says Abdul, "the rest of the story went down to the bottom of the river with the crocodile. It will take some time to get it up again. Before I see you again I will send somebody to find out about it, and let you know." Abdul has never come again; perhaps he is still looking for the news.

So much, then, for my travels in the palanquin. Outside the palanquin there were days when I assumed the role of a teacher,

and the railings of the verandah were my pupils. They were all afraid of me, and would cower before me in silence. Some of them were very naughty, and cared absolutely nothing for their books. I told them with dire threats that when they grew up they would be fit for nothing but casual labour. They bore the marks of my beatings from head to foot, yet they did not stop being naughty. For it would not have done for them to stop, it would have made an end of my game.

There was another game, too, with my wooden lion. I heard stories of *pujā* sacrifices and decided that the lion would be a magnificent thing. I rained blows on his back—with a frail little stick. There had to be a *mantra*, of course, otherwise it would not have been a proper *pujā:*

"Liony, liony, off with your head,
Liony, liony, now you are dead.
Woofle the walnut goes clappety clap,
Snip, Snop, Snap!"

I had borrowed almost every word in this from other sources; only the word "walnut" was my own. I was very fond of walnuts. From the words "clappety clap" you can see that my sacrificial knife was made of wood. And the word "snap" shows that it was not a strong one.

SONGS

POEMS

LIFE

This world is beautiful. I do not want to die.
I wish to live in the life of man,
and have a place in his living heart,
as in a sunbright flowerful garden.
Oh, the ceaseless ripple of life on earth,
the meetings and partings so happy and sad!
With human joys and griefs I shall wreathe my song,
and live for ever in the deathless life of man.
If I fail, then may I have
a little place in your midst, my friends,
and make new songs at morn and eve,
like flowers that bloom to be culled by you.
    Pick my flowers with a smile on your face,
    and throw them away when they fade.

1886

ON A RAINY DAY

On a day like this one could tell her.
On a day like this,
enveloped in rain and sunless,
dark and echoing with thunder.

None other shall hear.
All is lonely, all is dark.
Sit face to face, eyes looking into eyes.
The sky pours on without let,
the world seems bereft of all others.

The noises and the voices of the world
are unreal, distant, non-existent.
Only eyes drink in eyes,
only heart beats to heart.
Outside, all is merged in the dark.

Tell her, and the words will not sound rude.
Tell her, and the heart will not tremble.
Words will mingle with tears
and merge in the wind and the rain,—
One message will envelop two hearts.

What harm to any should come
if on this *Shravan* day laden with rain
I lighten my heavy heart
in this lost corner of the world?
Why, it should matter to none.

There will remain the whole of the year
for people's laughter and disdain.
Men will come and go,
there will be sorrow and pain
and life will go on for ever.

Today the wind blows restless
and lightning flashes from the sky.
Today in this pouring, deep, dark rain,
one could tell her things
that have always lurked in the mind.

1889

2000 A.D.

Who are you, reader, reading my poems an
hundred years hence?

I cannot send you one single flower
from this wealth of the spring, one single streak of gold
from yonder clouds.

Open your doors and look abroad.

From your blossoming garden gather fragrant
memories of the vanished flowers of an hundred
years before.

In the joy of your heart may you feel
the living joy that sang one spring morning,
sending its glad voice across an hundred years.

1896

A HALF-ACRE OF LAND

I had forfeited all my land except for one half-acre.
The landlord said, "Upen, I'll buy it, you must hand it over."
I said, "You're rich, you've endless land, can't you see
That all I've got is a patch on which to die?"
"Old man," he sneered, "you know I've made a garden;

If I have your half-acre its length and breadth will be even.
You'll have to sell." Then I said with my hands on my heart
And tears in my eyes, "Don't take my only plot!
It's more than gold—for seven generations my family
Has owned it: must I sell my own mother through poverty?"
He was silent for a while as his eyes grew red with fury.
"All right, we'll see," he said, smiling cruelly.
Six weeks later I had left and was out on the road;
Everything was sold, debt claimed through a fraudulent deed.
For those want most, alas, who already have plenty:
The rich *zamindār* steals the beggar-man's property
I decided God did not intend me for worldliness:
In exchange for my land he had given me the universe.
I became disciple to a *sādhu*—I roamed the world:
Many and pleasing were the sights and places I beheld.
But nowhere on mountain or sea, in desert or city could I wander
Without thinking, day and night, of that half-acre.
Roads, markets, fields—over fifteen years went past;
But finally my homesickness grew too great to resist.

I bow, I bow to my beautiful motherland Bengal!
To your river-banks, to your winds that cool and console;
Your plains, whose dust the sky bends down to kiss;
Your shrouded villages, that are nests of shade and peace;
Your leafy mango-woods, where the herd-boys play;
Your deep ponds, loving and cool as the midnight sky;
Your sweet-hearted women returning home with water;
I tremble in my soul and weep when I call you Mother.
Two days later at noon I entered my native village:
The pottery to the right, to the left the festival carriage;
Past temple, market-place, granary, on I came
Till thirsty and tired, at last I arrived at my home.

But shame on you, shame on you, shameless, fallen half-acre!
What mother gives herself freely to a chance seducer?
Do you not remember the days when you nursed me humbly
With fruits and herbs and flowers held in your sari?
For whom are these lavish garments, these languorous airs?
These coloured leaves stitched in your sari, this head of flowers?
For you I have wandered, homeless, world-weary, pining,
Whereas you, you witch, have sat here idling and laughing.
How a wealthy man's love has turned your head! How wholly
You have changed—all signs of the past have gone completely.
You cared for me before, you fed me, your bounty was abundant.
You were a goddess; now, for all your wiles, you are a servant.

As I paced with my heart in two I looked round and saw
There was still, near the wall, the same old mango-tree.
I sat at its foot and soothed my pain with tears,
And memories rose in my mind of childhood days:
How after a storm that had kept me awake one night
I had dashed out at dawn to gather all the fallen fruit;
Memories of playing truant in the sweet, still noon—
Alas to think those days can never return.
Suddenly a sharp gust of wind shook the branches above me
And two ripe mangoes fell to the ground beside me.
I mused: my mother still knows her son, maybe.
I took that gift of love, reverently touched it to my brow.
Then the gardener appeared from somewhere, like a messenger of death—
A topknotted *Oriyā*, abusing me for all he was worth.
I said, "I gave away everything with scarcely a murmur,
And now when I claim two mangoes there is all this uproar."
He didn't know me, he led me with a stick at his shoulders;
The landlord, rod in hand, was fishing with his retainers.
When he heard what had happened he roared, "I'll kill him."
In each vile thing he said his retainers exceeded him.
I said, "Two mangoes are all I beg of you, master."
He sneered, "He dresses as a *sādhu* but he's a pukka robber."
I wept, but I laughed as well at the irony of life—
For he was now the great *sādhu*, and I was the thief.

1896

UNWORTHY GIFT

Far below flowed the Jumna, swift and clear, above
frowned the jutting bank.
Hills dark with the woods and scarred with the
torrents were gathered around.

Govinda, the great Sikh teacher, sat on the rock
reading scriptures, when Raghunath, his disciple, proud
of his wealth, came and bowed to him and said, "I have
brought my poor present, unworthy of your acceptance."

Thus saying he displayed before the teacher a pair of
gold bangles wrought with costly stones.
The master took up one of them, twirling it round
his finger, and the diamonds darted shafts of light.
Suddenly it slipped from his hand and rolled down
the bank into the water.
"Alas," screamed Raghunath, and jumped into the
stream.
The teacher set his eyes upon his book, and the water
held and hid what it stole and went its way.
The daylight faded when Raghunath came back to
the teacher tired and dripping.
He panted and said, "I can still get it back if you
show me where it fell."
The teacher took up the remaining bangle and throwing
it into the water said, "It is there."

1896

FIRST KISS

The skies lowered their eyes and grew silent.
The birds ceased to sing.
The wind dropped, rippling waters stilled at once and forest murmurs faded in the heart of the forest.
The horizon came down on the silent earth along the lonely bank of the silent river in the still shadow of the evening.
At that instant, at the solitary silent window we kissed each other for the first time.
All at once evening bells rang out of the temple and filled the sky.
The eternal stars shivered and our eyes filled with tears.

July, 1897

INVENTION OF SHOES

Said King Habu, "Listen, Minister Gabu.
All last night I pondered
Why my feet should catch the dust
Whenever they touch the earth.
All you officials here,
For your salaries you only care;
To state affairs you pay no heed,
And let my earth soil my feet.
What unearthly goings-on in my state!
But I warn you all:
This must be remedied at once, or heads will fall."

The frightened Gabu into a cold sweat broke,
And nearly died of worry.
The pandits paled, the women wailed
And gave up cooking rice and curry.
All night long the courtiers try
In vain to wink an eye.
His tears down his grey beard streaming,
Gabu at the King's feet fell and said,
"How shall we kiss the dust of your feet
If your feet don't catch the dust?"

After thinking hard the King said, "True.
But first things are first
And last things you should do.
First remove the dust,
Then solve the problem you have posed.
Why do I keep you all and so many Dee Es Cees,
If for lack of dust on the earth
You can't kiss the dust of my feet?"

So Gabu brought the learned and the wise,
Foreign and native, from far and near.
They fixed their glasses
On the tips of their noses,
And after a long session of thinking tough,
And using up nineteen barrels of snuff,
They said, "If we carry out Your Majesty's desire,
The earth no longer any crops will bear."
The king said,"Then why are you here?"

After laying their heads again together,
Seventeen and a half lakhs of brooms they brought,
And gave every speck and spot
Of dust so great a clout,
And raised such a pother,
That the town was hid, the sun blotted out.
The dust blocked all noses, mouths and throats,
And of sneezing and coughing caused many a fit.
The King said, "To rid the earth of dust
They fill it with it."

Twenty-one lakhs of *bheesties* instantly ran
With skins slung on their backs;
Drained all rivers, lakes and ponds
Down to the mud,
And poured the water on the land,
Causing a flood.
Creatures aquatic for lack of water died,
Those terrestrial the art of swimming tried.
Boats got stranded in mid-river,
The country was hit by colds and fever.
The King said, "Lud,
The asses have turned the dust into mud."

In conference the pundits sat again,
Of the problem of dust the solution to find;
They racked their brains, but in vain,
And nearly went out of their minds.
"Cover the earth with matting," some said;
Some wanted it carpeted instead;
Some others advised the King to live in a room
Without a hole or a chink
In walls and roof,
And absolutely dust-proof.

The last advice the King found right.
But he was afraid his kingdom might
To ruin run,
If the dust to shun,
He shut himself in day and night.
So they advised him, all together,
To cover the earth with leather;
The dusty earth to pack
Within a leather sack;
And thus his name record
As the earth's sovereign lord.
The job, they said, would be done like a shot,
Once the right *chamar* he got.

Every one dropped the work on hand,
Sallied forth at once, and scoured the land.
Up and down they searched, in and around,
But the right *chamar*
Or the right leather nowhere found.
At last an old man,
Head of the *Chamar* clan,
His way very slowly made
To the King, and gently smiling said:
"I can show you, with your leave,
The easy way your object to achieve.
To cover the earth there is no need,
If you cover your own two feet."

The King could not see
How a solution so easy
Would be at all commensurate
With a problem so obdurate.
"Imprison the rascal, impale him,"
The courtiers continued to blather,
While at the King's feet seated,
The old man cased them in leather.
"The idea is mine, my brain has been picked",
The Minister declared,
As shoes were invented,
And the earth was spared.

1900

THE HERO

Say we made a journey, mother,
Roaming far and wide together—
    You would have a palanquin,
    Doors kept open just a chink,
    I would ride a red horse, clip
Clop-clip along beside you, lifting
    Clouds of red dust with my clatter.

Now, suppose it's getting darker,
Suddenly we're blocked by water—
    What a place, how bleak and wild,
    Not a man or beast in sight.
    You take fright, feel in your mind
We're lost. I tell you, 'Don't be frightened,
    Look, we'll take that dried-up river.'

What a thorny, thistly region—
All the cattle have been taken
    Under cover for the night.
    How the path we're taking winds,
    Darkness makes it hard to find—
Then suddenly I hear you crying,
    'Near the water, what's that lantern?'

Next thing shouts and yells surround us,
Figures closing in upon us—
    All four bearers fall away,
    Quake in bushes; you remain
    Crouched in fear, reciting names
Of gods, while I keep calmly saying,
    'I am here, no one shall harm us.'

Just imagine, *lāthi*-wielding
Long-haired desperate villains wearing
Jabā-flowers behind their ears—
'Stay right there,' I shout, 'keep clear!
See this sword? I'll chop you, pierce
Each man who comes one footstep nearer.'
Still they come, leaping and yelling.

You say, 'No, Oh don't go near them!'
I say, 'Sit tight, I can take them,
Watch—I spur my horse, at once
Swords and bucklers clash and thud—
Mother, you would faint at such
A fight! Some flee; the rest I scupper
Somehow: run them through, behead them.

You think they have surely killed me,
All those hefty men against me,
Till I roll up, smeared with blood,
Pouring sweat—'The battle's done,
Come outside,' I call. You rush
And hug me, kiss me. 'What a lucky
Thing,' you say, 'that you were with me.'

Life is such a boring matter,
Why are the exciting stories never
True? How this one would amaze
Neighbours, brothers—what? such great
Strength in one so small? My fame
Would spread, with everybody saying,
'What luck he was with his mother!'

1903

ON THE SEASHORE

On the seashore of endless worlds children meet. The infinite sky is motionless overhead and the restless water is boisterous. On the seashore of endless worlds the children meet with shouts and dances.

They build their houses with sand, and they play with empty shells. With withered leaves they weave their boats and smilingly float them on the vast deep. Children have their play on the seashore of worlds.

They know not how to swim, they know not how to cast nets. Pearl-fishers dive for pearls, merchants sail in their ships, while children gather pebbles and scatter them again. They seek not for hidden treasures, they know not how to cast nets.

The sea surges up with laughter, and pale gleams the smile of the sea-beach. Death-dealing waves sing meaningless ballads to the children, even like a mother while rocking her baby's cradle. The sea plays with children, and pale gleams the smile of the sea-beach.

On the seashore of endless worlds children meet. Tempest roams in the pathless sky, ships are wrecked in the trackless water, death is abroad and children play. On the seashore of endless worlds is the great meeting of children.

1903

IF NO ONE CALLS

If no one answers to your call
go your way alone.

If all are mute, oh! hapless one,
if all are filled with fear,
then open your heart in a fearless burst
and speak the truth alone.

If all go back, oh! hapless one,
when you are on your way
along the deep dark forest track,
if no one turns his face;
then walk the thorny path
with proudly bleeding feet,
with face set bravely forward
the bloodstained dust behind.

If no one lights the beacon
on a dark and stormy night;
if no one hears your knocking
and all men shut their doors:
then lose not heart oh! hapless one
but in the fiery thunder
set the torch of thy heart aflame
and burn in the dark alone.

1905

AUTHORSHIP

You say that father writes a lot of books, but what he writes I don't understand.
He was reading to you all the evening, but could you really make out what he meant?

What nice stories, mother, you can tell us! Why can't father write like that I wonder?
Did he never hear form his own mother stories of giants and fairies and princesses?
Has he forgotten them all?

Often when he gets late for his bath you have to go and call him an hundred times.
You wait and keep his dishes warm for him, but he goes on writing and forgets.
Father always plays at making books.

If ever I go to play in father's room, you come and call me, "What a naughty child!"
If I make the slightest noise you say, "Don't you see that father's at his work?"
What's the fun of always writing and writing?

When I take up father's pen or pencil and write upon his book just as he does,—a,b,c,d,e,f,g,h,i,—why do you get cross with me then, mother?
You never say a word when father writes.

When my father wastes such heaps of paper, mother, you don't seem to mind at all.
But if I take only one sheet to make a boat with, you say, "Child, how troublesome you are!"
What do you think of father's spoiling sheets and sheets of paper with black marks all over on both sides?

1909

GITANJALI
Verses XXII and XXIII

In the deep shadows of the rainy July, with secret steps, thou walkest, silent as night, eluding all watchers. To-day the morning has closed its eyes, heedless of the insistent calls of the loud east wind, and a thick veil has been drawn over the ever-wakeful blue sky. The woodlands have hushed their songs, and doors are all shut at every house. Thou art the solitary wayfarer in this deserted street. Oh, my only friend, my best beloved, the gates are open in my house—do not pass by like a dream.

Art thou abroad on this stormy night on thy journey of love, my friend? The sky groans like one in despair. I have no sleep to-night. Ever and again I open my door and look out on the darkness, my friend! I can see nothing before me. I wonder where lies thy path! By what dim shore of the ink-black river, by what far edge of the frowning forest, through what mazy depth of gloom art thou threading thy course to come to me, my friend?

1910

GRANDFATHER'S HOLIDAY

Blue sky, paddy fields, grandchild's play,
Deep ponds, diving-stage, child's holiday;
Tree shade, barn corners, catch-me-if-you-dare,
Undergrowth, *pārul*-bushes, life without care.
Green paddy all a-quiver, hopeful as a child,
Child prancing, river dancing, waves running wild.

Bespectacled grandfather old man am I,
Trapped in my work like a spiderwebbed fly.
Your games are my games, my proxy holiday,
Your laugh the sweetest music I shall ever play.
Your joy is mine, my mischief in your eyes,
Your delight the country where my freedom lies.

Autumn sailing in, now, steered by your play,
Bringing white *śiuli*-flowers to grace your holiday.
Pleasure of the chilly air tingling me at night,
Blown from Himālaya on the breeze of your delight.
Dawn in *Āśvin*, flower-forcing roseate sun,
Dressed in the colours of a grandchild's fun.

Flooding of my study with your leaps and your capers,
Work gone, books flying, avalanche of papers.
Arms round my neck, in my lap bounce thump—
Hurricane of freedom in my heart as you jump.
Who has taught you, how he does it, I shall never know—
You're the one who teaches me to let myself go.

1918

PALM-TREE

Palm-tree: single-legged giant,
topping the other trees,
peering at the firmament—
It longs to pierce the black cloud-ceiling
and fly away, away,
if only it had wings.

The tree seems to express its wish
in the tossing of its head:
its fronds heave and swish—
It thinks, Maybe my leaves are feathers,
and nothing stops me now
from rising on their flutter.

All day the fronds on the windblown tree
soar and flap and shudder
as though it thinks it can fly,
As though it wanders in the skies,
travelling who knows where,
wheeling past the stars—

And then as soon as the wind dies down,
the fronds subside, subside:
the mind of the tree returns
To earth, recalls that earth is its mother:
and then it likes once more
its earthly corner.

1922

Once again I wake up when the night has waned,
when the world opens all its petals once more,
and this is an endless wonder.
Vast islands have sunk in the abyss unknown,
Stars have been beggared of the last flicker
of their light,
countless epochs have lost all their cargo of things.
World-conquerors have vanished into the shadow of a name
behind dim legends,
great nations raised their towers of triumphs
as a mere offering to the unappeasable hunger
of the dust.
Among this immense crowd of the discarded
my forehead receives the consecration of light, —
and this is an endless wonder.
I stand for another day with the Himalayas,
with constellations of stars.
I am here where in the surging sea-waves
the infuriate dance of the Terrible is rhythmed with his boisterous
laughter.
The centuries on which have flashed and foundered
kingly crowns like bubbles
have left their signature on the bark of this aged tree,
Here I am allowed to sit under its ancient shade for one more day,
and this is an endless wonder.

Rabindranath Tagore

1932

আবার জাগিনু আমি।
রাত্রি হোলো ক্ষয়।
পাপড়ি মেলিল বিশ্ব
এই তো বিস্ময়
অন্তহীন।
ডুবে গেছে কত মহাদেশ,
নিবে গেছে কত তারা,
হয়েছে নিঃশেষ
কত যুগ যুগান্তর।
বিশ্বজয়ী বীর
নিজেরে বিলুপ্ত করি শুধু কাহিনীর
বাক্যপ্রান্তে আছে ছায়াপ্রায়।
কত জাতি
কীর্তিস্তম্ভ রক্তপাঁকে তুলেছিল যাঁরা
মিটাতে ধূলির মহাক্ষুধা।
সে বিরাট
ধ্বংসমাঝে অকস্মাৎ আমার ললাটে
পেলো অরুণের টিকা আরো একদিন
নিদ্রাশেষে,
এই তো বিস্ময় অন্তহীন।
আজ আমি নিখিলের জ্যোতিষ্কসভাতে
রয়েছি দাঁড়ায়ে।
আছি হিমাদ্রির সাথে,
আছি সপ্তর্ষির সাথে,
আছি যেথা সমুদ্রের
তরঙ্গ ভঙ্গিমা উঠে উদ্ধত রুদ্রের
অট্টহাস্য নাট্যলীলা।
এ বনস্পতির
বল্কলে স্বাক্ষর আছে বহু শতাব্দীর,
কত রাজমুকুটেরে দেখিল খসিতে।
তারি ছায়াতলে আমি পেয়েছি বসিতে
আরো একদিন—
জানি যে দিনের মাঝে
কালের রাখাল তবু ছাড়িয়ার বাজে॥

১২ আষাঢ়
১৩৩১

শ্রীরবীন্দ্রনাথ ঠাকুর

A QUESTION

O Lord,
Age after age,
Thou hast sent thy messengers to this pitiless world.
They proclaim:
'Remove all ill-will from your hearts,
Forgive and love.'
They are our masters,
And in reverence we cherish their memories.
Yet, on this evil day, I have turned them away
With an empty salutation.

I have seen:
Malice cunningly kill the helpless,
An insolent Might smother the voice of Justice,
Weeping in solitude!
I have seen:
Tender youth cry out in frenzied agony.
Dashing its head against the cold stone!

Today my voice is choked and mute is my flute—
My world has disappeared in an evil dream.
Therefore with tears I ask thee:
'Those who have poisoned thine air
And extinguished thy light,
Hast thou forgiven them?
Hast thou loved them?'

1932

AFRICA

In that bewildered Age
When the Creator, unsatisfied with his creation,
Destroyed it time and again,
The wrathful sea separated you, O Africa,
From the bosom of ancient earth,
And He girded you with dense forests
Impenetrable to light.
There, in your inmost recess,
You gathered the mysteries of the Incomprehensible.
And unravelled the riddle of
Earth, sky and water.
The magic of Nature, beyond the ken of human eye,
Was maturing its message beneath your consciousness.
O sun-shaded Africa!
Shrouded in a veil,
Under the turbid glance of contempt
Your humanity lay hidden.
On they came with shackles of iron,
These man-hunters—
Their claws sharper than tiger's,
Their minds dark with pride—
Darker than your sunless forest!
The cruel greed of the Civilized
Laid bare its shameless humanity;
The tracks of the forest,
Ringing with your wordless cry,
Became soiled with blood and tears.
The nailed boots of the plunderers
Left behind their indelible mark
On your dishonoured history.

At that very hour, beyond the seas,
The church bells rang calling men to prayer;
Children played on mothers' laps,
And in the poet's song
Rang the invocations to the Beautiful.
Today, when the night is choked with thunder,
And beasts emerge from hidden caves
Presaging the end of an Era,
Come, O Poet of a New Age—
Stand in the fading light of the dusk
Amongst the dishonoured,
And proclaim: "Forgive, O forgive!"
May this be your last message,
O Africa!

1938

SHORT STORIES

NOVELS

THE HUNGRY STONES

My kinsman and myself were returning to Calcutta from our *Puja* trip when we met the man in a train. From his dress and bearing we took him at first for an up-country Mahomedan, but we were puzzled as we heard him talk. He discoursed upon all subjects so confidently that you might think the Disposer of All Things consulted him at all times in all that He did. As we had never stirred out of our homes before, the demeanour of the man struck us dumb with wonder. Be the topic ever so trivial, he would quote science, or comment on the *Vedas*, or repeat quatrains from some Persian poet; and as we had no pretence to a knowledge of science or the *Vedas* or Persian, our admiration for him went on increasing, and my kinsman, firmly convinced that our fellow-passenger must have been supernaturally inspired by some strange "magnetism" or "occult power", listened to the tritest saying that fell from the lips of our extraordinary companion with devotional rapture, and secretly took down notes of his conversation.

When the train reached the junction, we assembled in the waiting-room for the connection. It was then 10 p.m., and as the train, we heard, was likely to be very late, owing to something wrong on the lines, I spread my bed on the table and was about to lie down for a comfortable doze, when the extraordinary person deliberately set about spinning the following yarn. Of course, I could not get to sleep that night.

★ ★ ★ ★ ★ ★ ★

When I threw up my post at Junagarh, and entered the service of the Nizam of Hyderabad, they appointed me at once, as a strong young man, collector of cotton duties at Barich.

Barich is a lovely place. The *Susta* "chatters over stony ways and babbles on the pebbles," tripping, like a skilful dancing girl, in through the woods below the lonely hills. A flight of one hundred and fifty steps rises from the river, and above that flight, on the river's brim and at the foot of the hills, there stands a solitary marble palace. Around it there is no habitation of man—the village and cotton mart of Barich being far off.

About two hundred and fifty years ago the Emperor Mahmud Shah II had built this lonely palace for his pleasure and luxury. In his days jets of rose-water spurted from its fountains, and on the cold marble floors of its spray-cooled rooms young Persian damsels would sit, their hair dishevelled before bathing, and, splashing their soft naked feet in the clear water of the reservoirs, would sing, to the tune of the guitar, the *ghazals* of their vineyards.

The fountains play no longer; the songs have ceased; no longer do snow-white feet step gracefully on the snowy marble. It is but the vast and solitary quarters of cess-collectors like us, men oppressed with solitude and deprived of the society of women. Now, Karim Khan, the old clerk of my office, warned me repeatedly not to take up my abode there. "Pass the day there, if you like," said he, "but never stay the night." I passed it off with a light laugh. The servants said that they would work till dark, and go away at night. I gave my ready assent. The house had such a bad name that even thieves would not venture near it after dark.

At first the solitude of the deserted palace weighed upon me like a nightmare. I would stay out, and work hard as long as possible, then return home at night jaded and tired, go to bed and fall asleep.

Before a week had passed, the place began to exert a weird fascination upon me. It is difficult to describe or induce people to believe; but I felt as if the whole house was like a living organism slowly and imperceptibly digesting me by the action of some stupefying gastric juice. I distinctly remember the day on which I first was conscious of it.

It was the beginning of summer, and the market being dull I had no work to do. A little before sunset I was sitting in an armchair near the water's edge below the steps. The *Susta* had shrunk and sunk low; a broad patch of sand on the other side glowed with the hues of evening; on this side the pebbles at the bottom of the clear shallow waters were glistening. There was not a breath of wind anywhere, and the still air was laden with an oppressive scent from the spicy shrubs growing on the hills close by.

As the sun sank behind the hill-tops a long dark curtain fell upon the stage of day, and the intervening hills cut short the time in which light and shade mingle at sunset. I thought of going out for a ride, and was about to get up when I heard a footfall on the steps behind. I looked back, but there was no one.

As I sat down again, thinking it to be an illusion, I heard many footfalls, as if a large number of persons were rushing down the steps. A strange thrill of delight, slightly tinged with fear, passed through my frame, and though there was not a figure before my eyes, I thought I saw a bevy of joyous maidens coming down the steps to bathe in the *Susta* in that summer evening. Not a sound was in the valley, in the river, or in the palace, to break the silence, but I distinctly heard the maidens' gay and mirthful laugh, like the gurgle of a spring gushing forth in a hundred cascades, as they ran past me, in quick playful pursuit of each other, towards the river, without noticing me at all. As they were invisible to me, so I was, as it were, invisible to them. The river was perfectly calm, but I felt that its still, shallow, and clear waters were stirred suddenly by the splash of many an arm jingling with bracelets, that the girls laughed and dashed and spattered water at one another, that the feet of the fair swimmers tossed the tiny waves up in showers of pearl.

I felt a thrill at my heart—I cannot say whether the excitement was due to fear or delight or curiosity. I had a strong desire to see them more clearly, but naught was visible before me. I thought I could catch all that they said if I only strained my ears; but however hard I strained them, I heard nothing but the chirping of the cicadas in the woods. It seemed as if a dark curtain of two hundred and fifty years was hanging before me, and I would fain lift a corner of it tremblingly and peer through, though the assembly on the other side was completely enveloped in darkness.

The oppressive closeness of the evening was broken by a sudden gust of wind, and the still surface of the *Susta* rippled and curled like the hair of a nymph, and from the woods wrapt in the evening gloom there came forth a simultaneous murmur, as though they were awakening from a black dream. Call it reality or dream, the momentary glimpse of that invisible mirage reflected from a far-off world, vanished in a flash. The mystic forms that brushed past me with their quick unbodied steps, and loud, voiceless laughter, and threw themselves into the river, did not go back wringing their dripping robes as they went. Like fragrance wafted away by the wind they were dispersed by a single breath of the spring.

Then I was filled with a lively fear that it was the Muse that had taken advantage of my solitude and possessed me—the witch had evidently come to ruin a poor devil like myself making a living by collecting cotton duties. I decided to have a good dinner—it is the empty stomach that all sorts of incurable diseases find an easy prey. I sent for my cook and gave orders for a rich, sumptuous *moghlai* dinner, redolent of spices and *ghee*.

Next morning the whole affair appeared a queer fantasy. With a light heart I put on a *sola* hat like the *sahebs,* and drove out to my work. I was to have written my quarterly report that day, and expected to return late; but before it was dark I was strangely

drawn to my house—by what I could not say—I felt they were all waiting, and that I should delay no longer. Leaving my report unfinished I rose, put on my *sola* hat, and startling the dark, shady, desolate path with the rattle of my carriage, I reached the vast silent palace standing on the gloomy skirts of the hills.

On the first floor the stairs led to a very spacious hall, its roof stretching wide over ornamental arches resting on three rows of massive pillars, and groaning day and night under the weight of its own intense solitude. The day had just closed, and the lamps had not yet been lighted. As I pushed the door open a great bustle seemed to follow within, as if a throng of people had broken up in confusion, and rushed out through the doors and windows and corridors and verandas and rooms, to make its hurried escape.

As I saw no one I stood bewildered, my hair on end in a kind of ecstatic delight, and a faint scent of *attar* and unguents almost effaced by age lingered in my nostrils. Standing in the darkness of that vast desolate hall between the rows of those ancient pillars, I could hear the gurgle of fountains splashing on the marble floor, a strange tune on the guitar, the jingle of ornaments and the tinkle of anklets, the clang of bells tolling the hours, the distant note of *nahabat*, the din of the crystal pendants of chandeliers shaken by the breeze, the song of *bulbuls* from the cages in the corridors, the cackle of storks in the gardens, all creating round me a strange unearthly music.

Then I came under such a spell that this intangible, inaccessible, unearthly vision appeared to be the only reality in the world—and all else a mere dream. That I, that is to say, *Srijut* So-and-so, the eldest son of So-and-so of blessed memory, should be drawing a monthly salary of four hundred and fifty Rupees by the discharge of my duties as collector of cotton duties, and driving in my dog-cart to my office every day in a short coat and *sola* hat, appeared to me to be such an astonishingly ludicrous illusion that I burst into a horse-laugh, as I stood in the gloom of that vast silent hall.

At that moment my servant entered with a lighted kerosene lamp in his hand. I do not know whether he thought me mad, but it came back to me at once that I was in very deed *Srijut* So-and-so, son of So-and-so of blessed memory, and that, while our poets, great and small, alone could say whether inside or outside the earth there was a region where unseen fountains perpetually played and fairy guitars, struck by invisible fingers, sent forth an eternal harmony, this at any rate was certain, that I collected duties at the cotton market at Barich, and earned thereby four hundred and fifty

Rupees per mensem as my salary. I laughed in great glee at my curious illusion, as I sat over the newspaper at my camp-table, lighted by the kerosene lamp.

After I had finished my paper and eaten my *moghlai* dinner, I put out the lamp, and lay down on my bed in a small side-room. Through the open window a radiant star, high above the Avalli hills skirted by the darkness of their woods, was gazing intently from millions and millions of miles away in the sky at Mr. Collector lying on a humble camp-bedstead. I wondered and felt amused at the idea, and do not know when I fell asleep or how long I slept; but I suddenly awoke with a start, though I heard no sound and saw no intruder—only the steady bright star on the hill-top had set, and the dim light of the new moon was stealthily entering the room through the open window, as if ashamed of its intrusion.

I saw nobody, but felt as if someone was gently pushing me. As I awoke she said not a word, but beckoned me with her five fingers bedecked with rings to follow her cautiously. I got up noiselessly, and, though not a soul save myself was there in the countless apartments of that deserted palace with its slumbering sounds and waking echoes, I feared at every step lest any one should wake up. Most of the rooms of the palace were always kept closed, and I had never entered them.

I followed breathless and with silent steps my invisible guide —I cannot now say where. What endless dark and narrow passages, what long corridors, what silent and solemn audience-chambers and close secret cells I crossed!

Though I could not see my fair guide, her form was not invisible to my mind's eye—an Arab girl, her arms, hard and smooth as marble, visible through her loose sleeves, a thin veil falling on her face from the fringe of her cap, and a curved dagger at her waist! I thought that one of the thousand and one Arabian Nights had been wafted to me from the world of romance, and that at the dead of night I was wending my way through the dark narrow alleys of slumbering Bagdad to a trysting-place fraught with peril.

At last my fair guide stopped abruptly before a deep blue screen, and seemed to point to something below. There was nothing there, but a sudden dread froze the blood in my heart—I thought I saw there on the floor at the foot of the screen a terrible negro eunuch dressed in rich brocade, sitting and dozing with outstretched legs, with a naked sword on his lap. My fair guide lightly tripped over his legs and held up a fringe of the screen. I could catch a glimpse of a part of the room spread with a Persian carpet—some one was sitting inside on a bed—I could not see her, but only caught a glimpse of two exquisite feet in gold-embroidered slippers, hanging out from loose saffron-coloured *paijamas* and placed idly on the orange-coloured velvet carpet. On one side there was a bluish crystal tray on which a few apples, pears, oranges, and bunches of grapes in plenty, two small cups, and a gold-tinted decanter were evidently awaiting the guest. A fragrant intoxicating vapour, issuing from a strange sort of incense that burned within, almost overpowered my senses.

As with trembling heart I made an attempt to step across the outstretched legs of the eunuch, he woke up suddenly with a start, and the sword fell from his lap with a sharp clang on the marble floor.

A terrible scream made me jump, and I saw I was sitting on that camp-bedstead of mine sweating heavily; and the crescent moon looked pale in the morning light like a weary sleepless patient at dawn; and our crazy Meher Ali was crying out, as is his daily custom, "Stand back! Stand back!!" while he went along the lonely road.

Such was the abrupt close of one of my Arabian Nights; but there were yet a thousand nights left.

Then followed a great discord between my days and nights. During the day I would go to my work worn and tired, cursing the bewitching night and her empty dreams, but as night came my daily life with its bonds and shackles of work would appear a petty, false, ludicrous vanity.

After nightfall I was caught and overwhelmed in the snare of a strange intoxication. I would then be transformed into some unknown personage of a bygone age, playing my part in unwritten history; and my short English coat and tight breeches did not suit me in the least. With a red velvet cap on my head, loose *paijamas*, an embroidered vest, a long flowing silk gown, and coloured handkerchiefs scented with *attar*, I would complete my elaborate toilet, sit on a high-cushioned chair, and replace my cigarette with a many-coiled *albola* filled with rose-water, as if in eager expectation of a strange meeting with the beloved one.

I have no power to describe the marvellous incidents that unfolded themselves as the gloom of the night deepened. I felt as if in the curious apartments of that vast edifice the fragments of a beautiful story, which I could follow for some distance, but of which I could never see the end, flew about in a sudden gust of the vernal breeze. And all the same I would wander from room to room in pursuit of them the whole night long.

Amid the eddy of these dream-fragments, amid the smell of *henna* and the twanging of the guitar, amid the waves of air charged with fragrant spray, I would catch like a flash of lightning the momentary glimpse of a fair damsel. She it was who had saffron-coloured *paijamas*, white ruddy soft feet in gold-embroidered slippers with curved toes, a close-fitting bodice wrought with gold, a red cap, from which a golden frill fell on her snowy brow and cheeks.

She had maddened me. In pursuit of her I wandered from room to room, from path to path among the bewildering maze of alleys in the enchanted dreamland of the nether world of sleep.

Sometimes in the evening, while arraying myself carefully as a prince of the blood-royal before a large mirror, with a candle burning on either side, I would see a sudden reflection of the Persian beauty by the side of my own. A swift turn of her neck, a quick eager glance of intense passion and pain glowing in her large dark eyes, just a suspicion of speech on her dainty red lips, her figure, fair and slim, crowned with youth like a blossoming creeper, quickly uplifted in her graceful tilting gait, a dazzling flash of pain and craving and ecstasy, a smile and a glance and a blaze of jewels and silk, and she melted away. A wild gust of wind, laden with all the fragrance of hills and woods, would put out my light, and I would fling aside my dress and lie down on my bed, my eyes closed and my body thrilling with delight, and there around me in the breeze, amid all the perfume of the woods and hills, floated through the silent gloom many a caress and many a kiss and many a tender touch of hands, and gentle murmurs in my ears, and fragrant breaths on my brow; or a sweetly-perfumed kerchief was wafted again and again on my cheeks. Then slowly a mysterious serpent would twist her stupefying coils about me; and heaving a heavy sigh, I would lapse into insensibility, and then into a profound slumber.

One evening I decided to go out on my horse—I do not know who implored me to stay—but I would listen to no entreaties that day. My English hat and coat were resting on a rack, and I was about to take them down when a sudden whirlwind, crested with the sand of the *Susta* and the dead leaves of the Avalli hills, caught them up, and whirled them round and round, while a loud peal of merry laughter rose higher and higher, striking all the chords of mirth till it died away in the land of sunset.

I could not go out for my ride, and the next day I gave up my queer English coat and hat for good.

That day again at dead of night I heard the stifled heart-breaking sobs of someone—as if below the bed, below the floor, below the stony foundation of that gigantic palace, from the depths of a dark damp grave, a voice piteously cried and implored me: "Oh, rescue me! Break through these doors of hard illusion, deathlike slumber and fruitless dreams, place me by your side on the saddle, press me to your heart, and, riding through hills and woods and across the river; take me to the warm radiance of your sunny rooms above!"

Who am I? Oh, how can I rescue thee? What drowning beauty, what incarnate passion shall I drag to the shore from this wild eddy of dreams? O lovely ethereal apparition! Where didst thou flourish and when? By what cool spring, under the shade of what date-groves wast thou born—in the lap of what homeless wanderer in the desert? What Bedouin snatched thee from thy mother's arms, an opening bud plucked from a wild creeper, placed thee on a horse swift as lightning, crossed the burning sands, and took thee to the slave-market of what royal city? And there, what officer of the *Badshah*, seeing the glory of thy bashful blossoming youth, paid for thee in gold, placed thee in a golden palanquin, and offered thee as a present for the seraglio of his master? And O, the history of that place! The music of the *sareng*, the jingle of anklets, the occasional flash of daggers and the glowing wine of Shiraz poison, and the piercing flashing glance! What infinite grandeur, what endless servitude! The slave-girls to thy right and left waved the *chamar*, as diamonds flashed from their bracelets; the Badshah, the king of kings, fell on his knees at thy snowy feet in bejewelled shoes, and outside the terrible Abyssinian eunuch, looking like a messenger of death, but clothed like an angel, stood with a naked sword in his hand! Then, O, thou flower of the desert, swept away by the blood-stained dazzling ocean of grandeur, with its foam of jealousy, its rocks and shoals of intrigue, on what shore of cruel death wast thou cast, or in what other land more splendid and more cruel?

Suddenly at this moment that crazy Meher Ali screamed out: "Stand back! Stand back!! All is false! All is false!!" I opened my eyes and saw that it was already light. My *chaprasi* came and handed me my letters, and the cook waited with a *salaam* for my orders.

I said: "No, I can stay here no longer." That very day I packed up, and moved to my office. Old Karim Khan smiled a little as he saw me. I felt nettled, but said nothing, and fell to my work.

As evening approached I grew absent-minded; I felt as if I had an appointment to keep; and the work of examining the cotton accounts seemed wholly useless; even the *Nizamat* of the Nizam did not appear to be of much worth. Whatever belonged to the present, whatever was moving and acting and working for bread seemed trivial, meaningless, and contemptible.

I threw my pen down, closed my ledgers, got into my dog-cart, and drove away. I noticed that it stopped of itself at the gate of the marble palace just at the hour of twilight. With quick steps I climbed the stairs, and entered the room.

A heavy silence was reigning within. The dark rooms were looking sullen as if they had taken offence. My heart was full of contrition, but there was no one to whom I could lay it bare, or of whom I could ask forgiveness. I wandered about the dark rooms with a vacant mind. I wished I had a guitar to which I could sing to the unknown: "O fire, the poor moth that made a vain effort to fly away has come back to thee! Forgive it but this once, burn its wings and consume it in thy flame!"

Suddenly two tear-drops fell from overhead on my brow. Dark masses of clouds overcast the top of the Avalli hills that day. The gloomy woods and the sooty waters of the *Susta* were waiting in terrible suspense and in an ominous calm. Suddenly land, water, and sky shivered, and a wild tempest-blast rushed howling through the distant pathless woods, showing its lightning-teeth like a raving maniac who had broken his chains. The desolate halls of the palace banged their doors, and moaned in the bitterness of anguish.

The servants were all in the office, and there was no one to light the lamps. The night was cloudy and moonless. In the dense gloom within I could distinctly feel that a woman was lying on her face on the carpet below the bed—clasping and tearing her long dishevelled hair with desperate fingers. Blood was trickling down her fair brow, and she was now laughing a hard, harsh, mirthless laugh, now bursting into violent wringing sobs, now rending her bodice and striking at her bare bosom, as the wind roared in through the open window, and the rain poured in torrents and soaked her through and through.

All night there was no cessation of the storm or of the passionate cry. I wandered from room to room in the dark, with unavailing sorrow. Whom could I console when no one was by? Whose was this intense agony of sorrow? Whence arose this inconsolable grief?

And the mad man cried out: "Stand back! Stand back!! All is false! All is false!!"

I saw that the day had dawned, and Meher Ali was going round and round the palace with his usual cry in that dreadful weather. Suddenly it came to me that perhaps he also had once lived in that house, and that, though he had gone mad, he came there every day, and went round and round, fascinated by the weird spell cast by the marble demon.

Despite the storm and rain I ran to him and asked: "Ho, Meher Ali, what is false?"

The man answered nothing, but pushing me aside went round and round with his frantic cry, like a bird flying fascinated about the jaws of a snake, and made a desperate effort to warn himself by repeating: "Stand back! Stand back!! All is false! All is false!!"

I ran like a mad man through the pelting rain to my office, and asked Karim Khan: "Tell me the meaning of all this!"

What I gathered from that old man was this: That at one time countless unrequited passions and unsatisfied longings and lurid flames of wild blazing pleasure raged within that palace, and that the curse of all the heart-aches and blasted hopes had made its every stone thirsty and hungry, eager to swallow up like a famished ogress any living man who might chance to approach. Not one of those who lived there for three consecutive nights could escape these cruel jaws, save Meher Ali, who had escaped at the cost of his reason.

I asked: "Is there no means whatever of my release?" The old man said: "There is only one means, and that is very difficult. It will tell you what it is, but first you must hear the history of a young Persian girl who once lived in that pleasure-dome. A stranger or a more bitterly heart-rending tragedy was never enacted on this earth."

★ ★ ★ ★ ★ ★ ★ ★

Just at this moment the *coolies* announced that the train was coming. We hurriedly packed up our luggage, as the train steamed in. An English gentleman, apparently just aroused from slumber, was looking out of a first-class carriage endeavouring to read the name of the station. As soon as he caught sight of our fellow-passenger he cried, "Hello," and took him into his own compartment. As we got into a second-class carriage, we had no chance of finding out who the man was nor what was the end of his story.

The Home and the World (Satyajit Ray film from the novel).

GORA
(an excerpt) — Ch. XXIX

At this point in the novel a young man Binoy has just seen his friend Gora sentenced to a month's imprisonment by the Magistrate, for interfering with the police in the discharge of their duties. Lolita, who knows them both, refuses to go with her family to the Magistrate's house, where they had been invited to be in a play that evening. She decides to return alone to Calcutta, as a demonstration of her support of Gourmoham Babu (Gora) whom she now sees in a new light.

The steamer's siren was sounding repeatedly for the passengers to come aboard, till at length it was time for her to cast off, when, just as the sailors were on the point of raising the gangway planks, Binoy, who was standing on the upper deck, saw a Bengali lady hastening towards the boat. Her dress and figure resembled Lolita's, but at first Binoy could hardly believe his eyes. When, however, she came nearer there could no longer be any doubt. For a moment he thought that she had come to fetch him, but then he remembered that Lolita also had been against going to the Magistrate's house that night.

Lolita just managed to catch the steamer, and as the sailors were engaged in casting off, Binoy came hurrying down in great alarm to meet her.

"Let us go up on to the upper deck," she said.

"But the steamer is starting," exclaimed Binoy in dismay.

"I know that," replied Lolita, and without waiting for Binoy she went up the stairs.

The steamer started with its siren hooting, and Binoy, having found a chair for Lolita on the upper deck, looked at her with silent question in his eyes.

"I am going to Calcutta," explained Lolita, "I found I couldn't possibly stay on."

"And what do the others say?" asked Binoy.

"Up to now no one knows," said Lolita. "I left a note and they will know when they read it."

Binoy was taken aback at this exhibition of self-will on Lolita's part, and he began hesitatingly: "But—"

Lolita stopped him with: "Now that the steamer has started what is the use of saying 'But'? I don't see why, because I happen to have been born a girl, I should have to put up with everything without protest. For us, also, there are such words as possible and impossible, right and wrong. It would have been easier for me to commit suicide than to have taken any part in that play of theirs."

Binoy saw that what was done was done, and no good would now come of worrying as to whether it was good or bad.

After some moments of silence Lolita went on: "I have been very unfair to your friend, Gourmohan Babu. I don't know why, but somehow, from the time I first saw him and heard him talk, my mind has been set against him. He always spoke with such vehemence, and you all seemed to say 'Yes' to whatever he said, it used to make me angry. I never could bear to be forced into anything, whether by speech or action. But now I see Gourmohan Babu forces things on himself as well as on other people—that's real power—I've not seen another man like him."

Thus Lolita talked on, not only because of her contrition for the way she had misjudged Gora, but because misgiving about what she had done just now would persist in raising its head in her inner consciousness; nor had she been able to realise how awkward it would be to have Binoy as her sole companion on board the steamer; but knowing full well that the more shame you show the more shameful it all gets to be, she began to chatter away for all she was worth.

Binoy, however, was at a loss for words. He was thinking on the one hand of the trouble and insult which had befallen Gora at the hands of the Magistrate, and on the other of his own disgrace in having come here to perform at the house of that same Magistrate. Over and above this there was this awkward situation with Lolita. These had combined to render him speechless.

In the old days such foolhardiness on Lolita's part would have earned her his censure, but now he could not entertain any such feeling. In fact, mixed with his surprise at her escapade was a certain amount of admiration for her pluck, and there was further the joy at the thought that, out of the whole party, he and Lolita were the only ones who had shown any real feeling about the insult to which Gora had been subjected.

For this defiance of theirs Binoy alone of the two would not have to suffer any untoward consequences, but Lolita would have to taste its bitter fruit for many a long day to come. How strange that Binoy should always have considered this very Lolita to be against Gora. The more he pondered over it, the higher grew his admiration for her intolerance of wrong-doing, her courage of conviction, regardless of the dictates of mere prudence—so much so that he knew not how to contain his feelings.

He felt that Lolita had rightly looked down upon him as lacking in strength and courage of conviction. He would never have been able to thrust aside so boldly all considerations of praise and blame from his own people, in order to pursue what he himself considered the right course. How often had he failed to be his own true self for fear of displeasing Gora, or lest Gora should think him weak, and then had deceived himself by subtle argument into the belief that Gora's view was his own!

He realised how superior Lolita had proved herself to him in the independence of her intellect, and honoured her accordingly. He badly wanted to ask Lolita's pardon for the way he had so often misjudged and inwardly blamed her in the past,—but could think of no way of putting his feelings into words. The vision of womanhood which he had gained to-day in the light of the glory which Lolita's beautifully courageous act had cast round her, made him feel that his very life was indeed fulfilled.

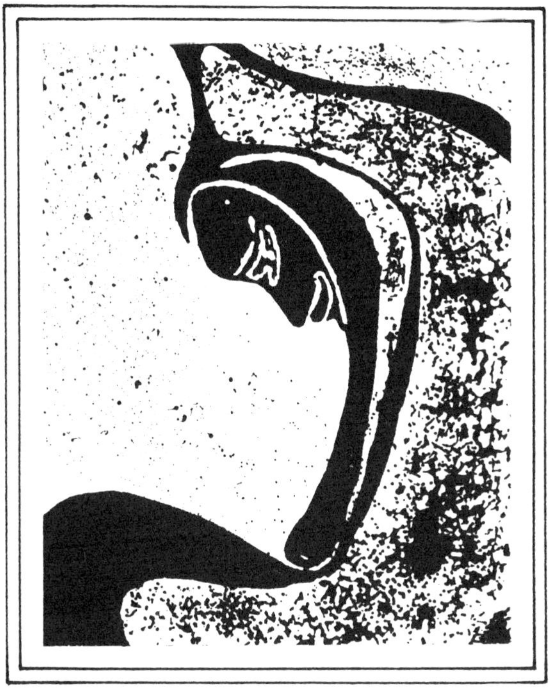

WRITINGS ON EDUCATION

THE STORY OF THE PARROT

There was once a bird that was stupid. It sang songs but did not know how to read the sacred books. It jumped, if flew about, but it knew no rules or etiquette.

The king said, "Such a bird is of no use; on the other hand as it feeds on wild fruit it serves no purpose for the royal fruit-market."

He called his minister and said, "The bird should be educated."

The responsibility of teaching the bird came to rest on the king's nephews. The pundits sat around to express their opinions. The question was, what was the reason of such ignorance on the part of the abovementioned bird?

The solution arrived at was that the nest which the bird built for itself with bits of dried straw was not the place for acquiring much knowledge. So that the first thing that was needed was a cage that should be suitably built. The king's learned men were showered with gifts and happily returned home.

The goldsmith started to build a golden cage. It was such an extraordinary cage that people came crowding from all places for learning. Others said, "Even if the bird does not learn anything it has at least the cage. How lucky the bird is!"

The goldsmith received a bagful of reward. With great delight he escaped to his home.

A pundit came to teach the bird. Sniffing his snuff he remarked, "This is not the work of merely a few books!"

The nephews then sent for the script-writers. They came and copied books and then copied the already copied books until the accumulated books were mountain-high. Whoever saw them said "Most admirable! Knowledge has no limit!"

The script-writers accepted remunerations which were piled up on a bullock's back. They wasted no time to hurry back home. Their days of hardship were over.

The nephews kept a constant watch over this expensive cage. There was always some repairing to be done and moreover when people noticed the elaborate method of dusting it, wiping it and polishing it, they remarked, "This, no doubt, is progress!"

To carry out this work a lot of people were needed, and to keep an eye on these people, yet more people had to be employed. They all got handsome monthly wages that mounted up in their safes.

They and their countless relations, near and dear, settled down happily in cushioned places in high buildings.

The world may be lacking in many other things, but critics who abound, are many. They said, "The cage is improving, but nobody seems to know what's happening to the bird!"

This reached the king's ears. He called one of his nephews and asked, "Dear nephew, what is this I hear?"

The nephew replied, "Your majesty, if you want to know the truth, send for the goldsmith, the pundits, the script-writers and also the people who do the repair-work and the supervisors. The fault-finders are starving that is why they must criticise!"

Satisfied with what he said the king came to understand the exact situation, and accordingly a gold necklace was hung round the nephew's neck.

The king expressed his wish that he would himself like to see this method of teaching which was so vigorously in practice. One day accompanied by his ministers, friends and advisers he came to visit the pupil.

At the entrance, music struck up all at once from every conceivable instrument—the conches, the bells, drums large and small, one-sided drums, kettle-drums, elongated drums, bell-metal instruments, flutes and cymbals. The pundits at the tops of their voices, shaking the tufts of hair on their otherwise shaven heads, started chanting the auspicious *slokas*. The mechanic, the work-man, the goldsmith, the copy-writer, the supervisor and moreover all the near and distant relatives of the king hailed him with shouts of welcome.

The nephew said, "Your Majesty, do you now see the extraordinary arrangement?"

The king replied, "It is marvellous! and the sounds of the music are no less impressive!"

The nephew replied, "It is not the sound only but the purpose behind it is just as meaningful!"

The king was pleased, and as he stepped out of the entrance to get up on his elephant, the fault-finder who had been hiding behind the bushes blurted out, "Your Majesty, have you seen the bird?"

The king was startled; he said "What a shame! I completely forget. I did not see the bird at all!"

He went back and saw the pundit and said, "How do you teach the bird, I must see the method!"

He saw it. He was extremely pleased. The method was so much greater than the bird itself that the bird was barely noticeable. It seemed there was no urgency that the bird should be seen. The king was convinced that there was no lack of preparations anywhere. There was no gram, no water in the cage, but page after page was being torn from stacks of piled-up books and with the pointed end of a pen they were shoved down the bird's throat. Its song was utterly smothered, and there was not even the tiniest gap through which the bird's cry, if there was any, could be audible. It was an astonishing affair!

When the king got up on his elephant this time, he warned the fault-finder that the punishing rod would be after-him.

Day by day the bird appeared more and more lifeless conforming to all rules of civilised respectability.

The guardians were convinced that everything was very hopeful. And yet due to an innate habit, the bird would look up to the morning light, and would unreasonably try to flutter its wings. Sometimes it was even seen that its thin beak would try to bite off the bars of the cage.

The police said, "This is the height of misbehaviour!"

Thereupon at the place where learning was in progress the blacksmith appeared with his furnace and his hammers. There went on a drastic hammering. An iron chain was made, the bird's wings were also clipped.

All the far and near relatives of the king with solemn looks, shook their heads as they passed their opinion "In this kingdom the birds have not only no sense, they are also ungrateful."

Then the pundit with a pen in one hand and a piercing rod in the other issued forth such rules that could only be justified in the name of education!

The blacksmith's reputation went up, gold jewellery covered his wife's body; and rewards were showered on the policeman, so pleased was the king with his vigilance!

The bird died. Exactly when nobody was able to say. The mischievous fault-finder spread the news, "The bird is dead."

The king called his nephew and asked, "Dear nephew, what is this I hear?"

The nephew replied, "Your Majesty, the bird received a complete education."

The king asked, "Did it hop any more?"

The nephew said, "That would have been a shame!"

"Did it fly any more?"
"No."
"Did it sing any more?"
"No."
"Did it screech when it did not get its gram?"
"No."
The king said, "Just bring over the bird, I would like to see it."

The bird was brought over. With it came the policeman, the footman, the men on horse-back. The king felt the bird with his hand. It made no sound, either hushed or loud. Only the dry pages of books made a rumbling and rustling noise in its stomach.

Outside in the south wind, the young leaves of the new spring breathed their sigh agitating the sky of the blossoming forest.

A POET'S SCHOOL

You have asked me to speak to you on my school and the principles which underline my method of teaching children. I founded my school twenty years ago, but, truly speaking, I had then neither method nor experience of teaching. I had gone ahead, however, in the confidence of having a kind of instinctive understanding of the child in which I have not been disappointed. Today I have undoubtedly acquired some experience but that experience is still, in a manner of speaking, fluid; it has not yet crystallized into a structure with sharp edges, the straight lines of which could be taken for guiding principles.

I have just told you when I started my school I had no experience whatsoever. That is not strictly correct. I had at least acquired a negative experience in the course of my own school-days. I had learnt how not to treat children. What I had particularly suffered in my childhood was to feel that the education that I had received was separated from life. I admit I had a certain special sensibility which others did not share with me in the same degree, otherwise I would undoubtedly have more easily resigned myself to my suffering, and would, in the course of those days at school, have succeeded like the others in stifling in me that passionate zest for life, for nature, from which every day I had to be dragged away as from a mother in order to enter the classroom.

I recall it, the door of the classroom, gaping each morning like a big mouth, its bare walls, its wooden benches, its wooden desk at which the teacher stood giving his lesson like a living phonograph. I still know it by heart, and I can hear it, the repetition of the same, which had neither the beauty of melody nor rhythm, which every morning we chanted in chorus on the wooden verandah of the school before entering the class. It spoke of many good things no doubt; that it was necessary to be wise, not to steal, nor borrow. But it was, nevertheless, a bad beginning for the day. I do not know how it is with your schools in the West; I do not know much about them, but I am told by people who should know, that all is not well with them either. I also know that it is to you that we owe these methods of education. You have brought them to us with many beautiful things; liquors, soldiers, etc., etc.

In that school, I learnt my grammar, my arithmetic, many things which I have completely forgotten, and how not to give lessons.

Thus when at the age of forty I felt the urge to come out of the little corner where I had lived in retirement until then on the banks of the Ganges and its sand flats, in order to do something useful, I resolved to teach children. It was not, however, that I believed that I had any special gift for teaching, but it seemed to me that I had the secret of making them happy.

To tell you the truth, nobody had any faith in me. I had neither a university degree, nor distinction of any kind. I passed for an extremely unpractical man, who knew nothing except writing verse. It was now a matter of finding blankets and sheets and of procuring food and lodging for the five boys who had been entrusted to my care.

I tried to live their daily life. Education, properly speaking, was a secondary matter. What was of the first importance was that our life was lived in common—our comradeship.

For me, indeed, a child up to his twelfth year lives much more in the subconscious than in clear consciousness and what is important during these first years is not to burden his memory with knowledge which taxes his mind, but to see that his subconscious is saturated with beauty through the contact of living nature.

In my school, I myself have never taught anything but languages and literature. I cannot produce any certificates for you but I can assure you that I taught them well. My pupils have told me they have never had a better language teacher. It goes without saying that I love words. A word for me is as living as a flower or a butterfly. Each word has its lustre, its sparkle, its subtle charm. That helped me to teach well all the languages that I know. I have had that experience with one pupil, my wife, whom I taught English in six months. An inspector of the University of Calcutta came to see me one day. He had seen me reading with my twelve-year-old boys Shelley's "Hymn to Intellectual Beauty" and he was surprised to see me reading with these children a text which is included in the curriculum of colleges and universities. Nevertheless, I do not believe in being able to make things childish in order to give them to children. I respect children and they understand me. It must be said also that I have been remarkably well supported. At the beginning of my school, a young poet of nineteen had voluntarily come forward to offer me his collaboration. If he had not died at the age of twenty, today he would have been one of the great poets of the world. He read Browning with his little pupils in a manner that made them feel the beauty of his poems. One can only teach what one loves. If one does not love what one teaches, one had better be silent. Also, you must teach only what has an element of mystery for you.

I have said this to my mathematician friends. They will able to teach the multiplication table well only if they love it. There are undoubtedly some who have a love for it. For me, it is inscribed in the petals of flowers and in the veins of leaves. Without knowning it, the butterflies carry it on their wings. I have said this to my friends, the mathematics teachers, and offered to share their teaching. They have shrugged their shoulders and dismissed my ideas as madness. It is probably because they are not poets just as I am not a mathematician. Nevertheless, I am convinced that one teaches best whatever has a touch of poetry for him.

Of course, I well know that one must make concessions to current orthodoxy. The children must go to universities; they must take the examinations, follow a curriculum. The parents "insist" on it. (The parents are their great enemies!) And since you must tread this road, you are lost . . .

When I teach anything, I always do it with love. I put myself heart and soul into it. And my friends tell me: "You could have obtained the same result with less effort; children must be given nourishment in rationed portions such as canned food." I know it well. But that is to kill the mind. We have had to do it in our school also. But I know that I am guilty of a crime. I hope that I shall be forgiven this in the other world, because truly I am not responsible for it alone, I have committed the crime in spite of myself.

As for me, I spent twelve years in the same school without ever receiving a prize. I have not had any prize except the Nobel Prize, but that too came late, when my days at school lay far behind me. Each year, all my friends brought books and other different things home as prizes. I never had anything, although my form master was one day moved to pity by my fate and asked the Headmaster to find out whether a prize could not be given to me all the same. The Headmaster had his moral scruples. "No," he said, "it wouldn't be fair, because he hasn't deserved one." But my teacher felt such pity for me (I wasn't unhappy at all) that he fetched a book which he himself had written on Bengali metre and gave it to me. Finding nothing else to say for this prize, he wrote on the fly leaf: "For good conduct." You should know this in order to realize that I had no right to talk of school and its curriculum.

For, indeed, I have never myself followed its curriculum. I should be incapable of passing an examination on my own poems, although my pupils, I feel sure, would score full marks.

Thus one leading principle, and one only, emanates from my ideas: Go to meet life where it is supreme. Come out of the school room. Do not bring trees into the classroom. Take the classes out under the trees. Undoubtedly, it is easy to have a tree trunk in the school room, it can be cut into planks; but these planks are dead, it is not in the classroom that the tree will bear flowers and fruit.

Do not be preoccupied with method. Leave your instincts to guide you to life. Children differ from one another. One must learn to know them, to navigate among them as one navigates among reefs. To explore the geography of their minds, a mysterious instinct, sympathetic to life, is the best of all guides.

FREE CURRENT
(an excerpt)

Ranajit, the Maharaja, and his Minister are talking together when they are interrupted by the entrance of the schoolmaster of Uttarakut, with his boys.

MASTER. You'll be getting a taste of the cane, I can see. Loudly now, shout, Jai! Rajarajeswar!
BOYS. Jai, Rajara . . .
MASTER. [*slapping a boy or two within his reach*] . . . jeswar!
BOYS. Jeswar!
RANAJIT. Where are you all going?
MASTER. Sire, your Majesty is to confer honour on our royal engineer Bibhuti, so I am taking the boys to share the rejoicings. They have learned from childhood to honour everything that is to the glory of Uttarakut. I don't want them to miss any opportunity.
RANAJIT. They all know, I suppose, what Bobhuti has done?
BOYS. [*jumping and clapping their hands*] Yes, yes, he has stopped up Shiv-tarai's drinking water.
RANAJIT. Why did he do that?
BOYS. To make them smart!
RANAJIT. And why should he make them smart?
BOYS. Because they are bad men.
RANAJIT. How bad?
BOYS. Everybody knows it, they are *very* bad, *awfully* bad.
RANAJIT. But you don't know why they are bad?
MASTER. Of course they know, Maharaja. Now, you, didn't you read? Didn't you read in your book? [*Whispering*] Their religion is very bad.
BOYS. Yes, yes, their religion is very bad.
MASTER. And besides, they are not like us. Come now, speak up! [*He points to his nose.*]

BOYS. They haven't got high-ridged noses.
MASTER. Right, now what has our professor proved? What does a high-ridged nose show?
BOYS. The greatness of our race!
MASTER. Good! And what will that great race do? Come, speak up! . . . they'll conquer . . . out with it, do! . . . they'll conquer everyone else in the world, won't they?
BOYS. Yes, everyone!
MASTER. Were the men of Uttarakut ever defeated in war?
BOYS. Never, never!
MASTER. Didn't our former king Pragjit, with two hundred and ninety-three men, drive back an army of thirty-one thousand seven hundred and ninety-three southern barbarians?
BOYS. Yes, yes!
MASTER. Rest assured, your Majesty, all these boys will be a terror one day to all wretched foreigners. If not, I am no true teacher. Not for a moment do I forget what a great responsibility is ours. It's we schoolmasters who mould men—your ministers have merely to use them. Yet think what a salary they get, compared with ours!
MINISTER. But these boys themselves are your reward.
MASTER. Well spoken, sir, the boys themselves *are* our reward. Alas, but food is dear. Just think; cow's *ghee*, which used to be . . .
MINISTER. All right, all right, I'll see about your *ghee*. Now go, it's nearly time for worship.
The schoolmaster goes out with his boys.
RANAJIT. This schoolmaster of yours has nothing in his head but *ghee*, cow's *ghee*.
MINISTER. There is certainly a good deal of the cow about him. But, Maharaja, fellows of this kind have their uses. Day after day they repeat, mechanically, exactly what they have been told. Things wouldn't run so smoothly if they had more sense.

ESSAYS

NATIONALISM
(an excerpt)

A nation, in the sense of the political and economic union of a people, is that aspect which a whole population assumes when organised for a mechanical purpose. Society as such has no ulterior purpose. It is an end in itself. It is a spontaneous self-expression of man as a social being. It is a natural regulation of human relationships, so that men can develop ideals of life in co-operation with one another. It has also a political side, but this is only for a special purpose. It is for self-preservation. It is merely the side of power, not of human ideals. And in the early days it had its separate place in society, restricted to the professionals. But when with the help of science and the perfecting of organisation this power begins to grow and brings in harvests of wealth, then it crosses its boundaries with amazing rapidity. For then it goads all its neighbouring societies with greed of material prosperity, and consequent mutual jealousy, and by the fear of each other's growth into powerfulness. The time comes when it can stop no longer, for the competition grows keener, organisation grows vaster, and selfishness attains supremacy. Trading upon the greed and fear of man, it occupies more and more space in society, and at last becomes its ruling force . . .

Have you not seen, since the commencement of the existence of the Nation, that the dread of it has been the one goblin-dread with which the whole world has been trembling? Wherever there is a dark corner, there is the suspicion of its secret malevolence; and people live in a perpetual distrust of its back where it has no eyes. Every sound of a footstep, every rustle of movement in the neighbourhood, sends a thrill of terror all round. And this terror is the parent of all that is base in man's nature. It makes one almost openly unashamed of inhumanity. Clever lies become matters of self-congratulation. Solemn pledges become a farce—laughable for their very solemnity. The Nation, with all its paraphernalia of power and prosperity, its flags and pious hymns, its blasphemous prayers in the churches, and the literary mock thunders of its patriotic bragging, cannot hide the fact that the Nation is the greatest evil for the Nation, that all its precautions are against it, and any new *birth of* its fellow in the world is always followed in its mind by the dread of a new peril. Its one wish is to trade on the feebleness of the rest of the world, like some insects that are bred in the paralysed flesh of victims kept just enough alive to make them toothsome and nutritious. Therefore it is ready to send its poisonous fluid into the vitals of the other living peoples, who, not being nations, are harmless. For this the Nation has had and still has its richest pature in Asia. Great China, rich with her ancient wisdom and social ethics, her discipline of industry and self-control, is like a whale awakening the lust of spoil in the heart of the Nation. She is already carrying in her quivering flesh harpoons sent by the unerring aim of the Nation, the creature of science and selfishness. Her pitiful attempt to shake off her traditions of humanity, her social ideals, and spend her last exhausted resources in drilling herself into modern efficiency, is thwarted at every step by the Nation. It is tightening its financial ropes round her, trying to drag her up on the shore and cut her into pieces, and then go and offer public thanksgiving to God for supporting the one existing evil and shattering the possibility of a new one. And for all this the Nation has been claiming the gratitude of history, and all eternity for its exploitation; ordering its band of praise to be struck up from end to end of the world, declaring itself to be the salt of the earth, the flower of humanity, the blessing of God hurled with all His force upon the naked skulls of the world of No-Nations.

CRISIS IN CIVILIZATION

The wheels of Fate will some day compel the English to give up their Indian Empire. But what kind of India will they leave behind, what stark misery? When the stream of their two centuries' administration runs dry at last, what a waste of mud and filth they will leave behind them! I had at one time believed that the springs of civilization would issue out of the heart of Europe. But today when I am about to quit the world that faith has gone bankrupt altogether.

Today I live in the hope that the Saviour is coming—that he will be born in our midst in this poverty-shamed hovel which is India. I shall wait to hear the divine message of civilization which he will bring with him, the supreme word of promise that he will speak unto man from this very eastern horizon to give faith and strength to all who hear.

As I look around I see the crumbling ruins of a proud civilization strewn like a vast heap of futility. And yet I shall not commit the grievous sin of losing faith in Man. I would rather look forward to the opening of a new chapter in his history after the cataclysm is over and the atmosphere rendered clean with the spirit of service and sacrifice. Perhaps that dawn will come from this horizon, from the East where the sun rises. A day will come when unvanquished Man will retrace his path of conquest, despite all barriers, to win back his lost human heritage.

Today we witness the perils which attend on the insolence of might; one day shall be borne out the full truth of what the sages have proclaimed:

अधर्मेणैधते तावत् ततो भद्राणि पश्यति ।
ततः सपत्नान् जयति समूलस्तु विनश्यति ॥

By unrighteousness man prospers, gains what appears desirable, conquers enemies, but perishes at the root.

April 1941

NOTES AND GLOSSARY

Letters from Europe: *Yurop-prabasir* (p. 15) translated by William Radice

zamindar — landowner

pugree — turban

Glimpses of Bengal: *chinnapatra* and *chinnapatrabali* (p. 19)

From the collection of letters, written during 1892-1896 when Tagore was looking after estates in Selaidah (now in Bangladesh). During that period the Poet often lived in a houseboat on the River Padma

Letter written to the Viceroy (p. 20) to renounce his knighthood following the massacre of unarmed civilians at Amritsar. The letter was published in the Indian press June 2nd

Letter to a friend (p. 21) written to C. F. Andrews, who is known as *Dinabandhu* (friend of destitutes) in India

My Boyhood Days: *chelebela* (p. 23) translated by Marjorie Sykes

hookāh — a type of pot for puffing tobacco

palanquin — covered litter for one carried by four or six men. In the 19th century it was a popular means of transport for rich people

durwan — gatekeeper

jamādār — a cleaner

sari — dress for Indian women

Rādhā — celebrated cowherdess beloved of Krishna

Krishna — god of Hindu mythology, incarnation of Visnu, often represented as blue in colour

Chaitra — last month of Bengali calendar, mid-March to mid-April

Vaíṡākh gale — a N.W. wind, often beginning hot weather during late April, early May

pakūd — tree (fig family)

ghāt — a restricted area of steps leading to the water where it is usual to bathe

pujā — ceremonial worship, both daily offerings and religious festivals come under this heading

mantra — chants

Songs and Poems (p. 31)

Where not stated the poems have been translated by the poet himself

Life: *Morite chahina āami* (p. 33)

2000 A.D.: *1400 Sal* (p. 37)

On a Rainy Day — *barshār dinē* (p. 34)

Shravan – fourth month of Bengali calendar, mid-July to mid-August
A Half-Acre of Land: *dui bighā jāmi* from *citra* (p. 38) translated by William Radice
zamindār – landowner
sadhu – a ascetic or merchant or respected man
Oriyā – a native of the state of Orissa, S. of India
Unworthy Gift: *nisphal upahār* (p. 40)
Jamunā – a river in N. India
Sikh – a community following the faith introduced by the great teacher Guru Nanak
First Kiss – *pratham chumban* (p. 41)
Invention of Shoes – *jutā ābiskār* (p. 42)
kiss the dust of my feet – a formal offering of reverence done by lightly touching the feet of the revered one and then one's own head with the same hand
bheesties – leather water carriers
chāmār – a shoemaker
King Habu and *Minister Gabu* are the stock fools of Bengali folklore
The Hero: *bīr-purus* from *śiśu* (p. 46) translated by William Radice
lathi – a stick for fighting, as policeman's baton
Jaba – hibiscus; bush with scarlet bell-shaped flowers
On The Seashore (p. 48) from *śiśu* and later from The Crescent Moon (Macmillan)
If No One Calls – *jadi toredāak shune* (p. 49) translated by Aruna Chakravarti
This song was Mahatma Gandhi's favourite and inspired him throughout his life
Gitanjali – *Song Offerings* (p. 51). The poet W. B. Yeats who became Tagore's friend, wrote a preface to the English publication of this work
Grandfather's Holiday: *thākur-dādār chuti* from *palātakā* translated by W. Radice (p. 52)
Palm-Tree: *tāl-gāch* from *śiśu bholānāth* translated by W. Radice (p. 53)
A Question: *praśna* (p. 56) from *parises* translated by Arabindo Bose
Africa: *āphrikā* (p. 57) from *patra-put* translated by Arabindo Bose
Short Stories/Novels (p. 59)
The Hungry Stones (p. 60) translated by Tagore himself
Puja holiday – festival, usually in October

Vedas — the Hindu scriptures, written in four parts
Susta — a river in S. India
ghazal — a popular form of poetry in Urdu, sometimes sung
cess-collector — tax collector
moghlai — derived from Moughal — ruler of India before the British
ghee — clarified butter used in Indian cooking
sola — light, softwood from an aquatic plant
sāhebs — an expression meaning British or other white-skinned males
āttar — a perfume
nahabat — an orchestra
bulbul — singing bird
srijut — Mr
paijamas — loose trousers worn in India
ālbolā — a form of hubble-bubble; smoke drawn through a long pipe
henna — scented flower; also a dye
Badshah — Muslim Emperor
sareng — a sort of violin
chamar — a yak-tail, used as a fan
chaprasi — a servant
salaam — a salute or greeting
Nizamat — Royalty
coolies — porters

The Home and the World — Satyajit Ray film from the novel (p. 71). This story is available in Penguin Modern Classics: Rabindranath Tagore: *The Home and the World* — introduced by Anita Desai. Set on a Bengali noble's estate in 1908, it is both a love story and a novel of political awakening

Gora (an excerpt) Ch. XXIX (p. 72) translation revised by Surendranath Tagore

Gora (1909), a socio-political novel, narrates the story of a man, who unknown to himself was born of Irish parents, but brought up as a Hindu. The story, Gora's love for a Brahmo girl, is told in the background of the intellectual debates of the time-religion, nationalism and feminism. This short excerpt reflects Tagore's strong convictions about women's rights and their place in society

The Story of the Parrot (*Totākāhini*) (p. 77)

This is a satire on the education system, translated by Krishna Kripalini *slokas* — couplets

A Poet's School (p. 80)

Translated by Sasadhar Sinha from "L'Educateur" No. 12, June 11 1921, from a talk given at L'Institut J. J. Rousseau in Geneva

Free-current (Muktadhārā) (p. 85)

This is an excerpt of an allegorical play translated by Marjorie Sykes. In this drama the king of 'Uttarakut' has been trying to enforce his subjection completely over the neighbouring state of 'Shiv-tarāi' by erecting a huge dam to prevent the waters of Muktadhārā from reaching the plains of 'shiv-tarāi'. The excerpt below shows clearly how the state-education has been influenced by the ulterior motives of the ruling class

Nationalism (p. 89)

An excerpt from a series of essays incorporated in the book 'Nationalism'

Crisis in Civilization (p. 90)

This is an excerpt from the Poet's last address on his birthday at Santiniketan in 1941

RECOMMENDED READING

Selected Poems: Rabindranath Tagore translated by William Radice (Penguin 1985, 1987)

Collected Poems and Plays of Rabindranath Tagore (Macmillan 1936 . . . 1983)

Rabindranath Tagore: A Biography by Krishna Kripalani (Oxford 1962)